The Bear & Dragon Saga

by Chris Carmines

Includes:
The Bear & Dragon Tales
Adventures of Bear & Dragon 1

Table of Contents

Dedication
For Little Bear and Yorkshire, my magical little storytellers.

Prologue

This is a story that I was told. I did not invent it; I did not conjure it. I am merely its scribe. It was gifted to me, one day, by my truest friend – a teddy bear who had found me while I was in graduate school. In honor of him I have presented his story exactly as he presented it to me. It is a true fairy tale, told often in rhyme, which is his way of speaking. It is not mine.

THE BEAR & DRAGON TALES

... Told by Little Bear

'Dragons are not real,' she said, more to the air than me. I was once her dearest friend. That she'd promised me. Alas, she'd grown up you see. I'd become old - just fuzz and foam – nothing very dear, I fear.

She fluffed a pillow to set me there. Without saying goodbye, I was left to stare. No longer her favored teddy bear, she did not await my reply. She shut the door instead.

My eyes could only widen. It would be impolite to declare, to shout out in fact, that I had known a dragon. Yes, a real dragon I had known, when I was just a bear cub.

That was long ago, and we're still friends. So long ago, that she'd not know, though I recall our story well. It was a time you see, when teddy bears were grizzly bears and dragons breathed bright fire.

In my time, I've gone from hand to hand and watched the world change. Yet none have seen what I have seen and wish to tell it still. So sit me in your lap just now and listen while I speak. I'll tell you of a time before, before our wonders hid.

I was just a baby cub; they called me Little Bear. In my wood lived all sorts of folk, some you'll know and some you'll not. With forest elves and water sprites, *futterblys,* oops, I mean butterflies and flower Faes...

"A Fae?" you say. A fairy—many kinds are they. Some live in flowers, some in trees, some in waterfalls, others dwell in caves. Most live in a land that people kind cannot find. That was not always so, as my story will show. Let me return to what I was to say.

With flower Fae and sky flits, the small *wingies* some call 'birds', 'bats', or 'moths', with air wisps known as *Sylphs* and four-leg kind, like me, with unicorns and shiny things – oh, with caterpillars too, ants and bugs and crawly things, with many things did I once live. I ate a lot and loved the smells. It was different then than now.

The people had not come, you see. So all of us, who are special folk, still spoke. We could be what we are, not what you think you see—that, the fairy glamour caused.

What is fairy glamour? You no longer know. Oh, pardon me; it's become something special indeed.

People folk think glamour is make-believe. It is not. Glamour is a trick the Fae folk played to keep us safe. Read on, please, you'll see. I'll tell you why the fairy glamour came to be. Yet first I'll tell you about my dragon friend and me. We were sort of a special key, for all that would come to be.

CHAPTER 1

One day I was out wandering. I did that every day. I fished for breakfast and went to roll down my favorite hill. As I stood on the crest, a yellow *futterbly* landed on my nose. It made me sneeze. I sneezed again, so hard that I fell down the hill. I rolled clear to the stream and splashed into the water.

Just then a voice said, "What are you?"

I climbed out of the stream and shook the water from my ears. I looked to see a something – a green lizard with wings – perched on a rock. It was a little something – little like me. Yet it was still a green lizard with wings – not like me – and it talked.

I never saw a four-leg with wings before. It had probably never seen a four-leg with fur before. I thought I'd better answer.

"Well I'm a bear, a little bear," I said.

"I'm a dragon, a little dragon. I breathe fire. Can you breathe fire?" the creature asked. It seemed very friendly, and just as curious as I.

"No, bears don't breathe fire; we fish," I answered.

"Then let's fish. You catch 'em. I'll cook 'em," the little dragon replied. I laughed.

"By the way, my name is Yorkshire; what's yours?" he asked.

"I'm Little Bear. I'm very pleased to meet you," I then shook Yorkshire's clawed paw.

"Your name is what you are," he said. "Then I'll be Little Dragon. I'm testing out my fire today, so meeting you is perfect. I was wondering what to do. I don't fish, you see."

"Oh, then I must teach you. You do eat fish, don't you?" I asked.

Uh-oh, I had no idea what dragons ate. I hoped it wasn't bears.

Yorkshire shook his head and said, "I love fish. My mother cooks them for me."

"I eat mine raw. I'll try them cooked," I added, hoping to be polite.

"Raw – oh dear, you don't eat dragons do you?" Yorkshire's eyes got big.

"Heavens, no!" I exclaimed, "I've never met a dragon."

We fished that afternoon. Yorkshire was right about his fire; we burned a few. Though done just right, cooked fish is good too. I shall tell my mother. Yorkshire says he'll come show her, if she'd like him to.

CHAPTER 2

That night I told my parents all about my newfound friend. My father says dragons are a noble breed, older even than bears. They were made from lightning and lava.

Lava is like fiery jam bubbling up from the soul of mountains. It is the home of fire beings, once called *Salamanders*, he said. I thought it very special to be made of lightning and dessert. I listened while my father spoke.

"Long ago it was dragons that allowed all we see to be. The *fire folk*, ever hungry, always moving, escaped their deep homes. Invading the surface, nothing else could live. Even water turned to air. All the earth was a fiery jam."

I guess that was very tasty, for a fire folk. They aren't mean, you see. Father says they do not imagine, do not see. Unlike you or me, they do not think. I suppose it's very tiring being a fire folk.

"Water beings, called *Undines* or even *water jinn*, their palaces dry, fled to the Ancient Ones." My father continued, "To the Great Thunders each one pled: 'please, please – save our home'. You see, even before long ago, the Thunders made all that we know.

"Wise beyond any, the Ancient Ones knew about balance," said father. "The water jinn had to be restored, but how? The fire flits too needed a home, yet had taken water's. With great care a solution was thought – a special vessel to host the invading fire folk. This new vessel –

a creature it was, made in the heavens, could travel the skies. Gifted with wings, wisdom and woe, by 'dragon' it was known.

"Hidden deep within dragon's skin, fire jinn could fly from lava pits to starry skies – a thing no jam could do. Enchanted and free the fire beings withdrew. The land was healed, never to be burnt again. Well – not without the Thunders permission 'twas told."

Father paused for effect, "The Undines cheered. Mists, springs, creeks, lakes, selkies, mermaids – even the ghosts of oceans past, overflowed the Thunders' halls. A flood of delight fell to earth. Water's gladness we call 'rain'.

"Rain blessed the dragons. No longer just lava and light, dragons became the land they saved. Each wore the color of the dirt it restored. There were black dragons, brown, red and yellow ones too, lilac, white, green and blue.

"Thereby the water folk cheered. They, with the Thunders, had made the dragons for the fire folk. Now, if you've ever seen a rainbow, you know just what I mean. Within its color bands, Salamanders with Undines play linking sky to land. Rainbows too our Thunders made. For as my mother told, once and long ago, all creation was for beauty and balance to hold.

"Indeed, that is the master plan. Yet, until all becomes pretty it never shall be done. My mother said to me, "That is called *Alchemy*".

Father leaned back, "Now that I'm an elder bear, even older than my father was then, when I look at what I see, I often wonder: Is there alchemy? Yes, there is. My cub days made me certain. There was great beauty then, and if I tell you of it, perhaps you'll find it again."

CHAPTER 3

Balance is the first thing I had to learn. If you recall, I'd fallen down a hill. Because of a futterbly, a dragon I met.

We played and talked and ate a bunch. He did not tell me what my father would. Not even when we were older did he speak. Perhaps remembering would have made him weep.

Many things I have not told you yet, he had seen. So if you ever meet a dragon, please understand, even the noblest of beings can be cast to ground.

I've probably lost you, haven't I? My apologies, so much happened, so much changed. I was only just learning to use my four feet, which is trickier than you think.

My front ones I could see; my back ones I forgot. If I went to look, over my front ones I would trip. Then on my back ones I would stand and my front ones I would lose. I became very confused. I sat down a lot.

My mother said I thought too much. My father told me "practice." That is why every day I wandered about, you see. I was getting better, though still I could not run. That I learned from my dragon friend. He taught me the nature of pretend.

"Do you believe in what you can not see?" he asked me, one day.

"Wind I've never seen, yet it blows dandelions away. I've never seen the North or South, the East or even West. The stars and sun have seen those directions, I guess. I've never seen below, below or above, above either. Yet stories of both I've certainly heard told. Yes – I believe in things I can not see."

"Good. Then catch me," Yorkshire said running off across the meadow.

"Wait!" I yelled. On four legs I couldn't run. I tried and fell and hit a rock. It hurt. I sat down and wished to cry. It was no use. I'd walk all my life.

Little dragon flew back to me. "Are you hurt?" he asked.

"No, and yes. I've never run. I don't know how, you see." I hid my face behind my paws.

"Don't worry. I'll teach you." Yorkshire flapped his wings, "Pretend it's going to work and it will."

I had no idea what he was speaking of.

"Stand up, up on your back legs and hold my tail. Close your eyes and follow me," he instructed, walking off.

I grabbed his tail and followed. Faster and faster he went. I felt scared and giddy too. I skipped along, then ran, chasing after my friend.

Yorkshire swished his tail; I lost my grip. Falling onto my front legs, my back legs came behind, lifting and pushing me on. My front legs reached out, my back legs followed; I was running on four legs and didn't know how. Yorkshire was right. By pretending I could, I did.

I leapt over bluebells, past tree frogs and squirrels. The ravens flew off, probably to tell my mother.

Yorkshire stopped, turning back to look. "I thought you couldn't run," he teased.

"I can't. It's only pretend. If I think, I'll fall down again."

Yorkshire laughed. "You're a very smart little bear. Listen to what you've said. What you feel is as vital as what you see. You ran with me, and could not see. You decided what would happen and made it be. Bravo!" Yorkshire breathed out a little blue flame and flapped his wings.

I was so lucky. What a wonderful new friend had come to me. I couldn't wait to show my parents; I can run!

CHAPTER 4

Mother was very proud, even though I surprised her quite a bit. I ran up behind her and pounced. "My goodness Little Bear, you are growing up!"

When I told her Yorkshire taught me, she smiled. "Why don't you two bring me fish for lunch tomorrow?"

I was very excited. Now I could fish and run. I couldn't make fire though. So I watched while Yorkshire made us a very special dish.

It was from the beginning times of dragon kind. Inside a great cauldron, ocean fruit bathed in water jinn's cheer; that means – fish in rainwater appeared. Kissed by Salamanders, the giant cauldron boiled and bubbled, frothed and fumed into the dragon's first meal – a secret potion the Thunders called *stew*.

By adding more cheer, a lovely tonic appeared. We call it *soup*. Yet if I put in earth fruit, or berries to people folk, and let the Salamanders play, one of my favorites is made. It is *jam*, you'd say.

Yorkshire does not care for berries though. He likes four-leg soup – that's what big dragons eat. I told him I did not want to hear. So instead our dish was made of fish.

My father came home for lunch and met my dragon friend. He told us both of times I'd not heard about. Yorkshire knew all about how dragons came to be. Neither of us knew what happened next. That is what my father told.

Being a creative kind, the Undines drizzled the waters with life. Whole carnivals of sprites swam beneath the ocean's waves. The dragons, high upon their mountaintops, felt lonely – and a little worried too. For you see, water was becoming as fire used to be. The earth had gone from jam to soup.

"Oh dear, what should we do?" The dragons thought to make a stew.

Their fiery breath blessed the borders, where sea and soil met. From the drying mists new beings did pop, creatures of air, the Sylphs of people's myths. Born of water and fire their natures were of both, yet unlike either. Dragon fire sparked them; ocean froth reflected them. Sylphs had lightning's speed and water's kind caress.

From the water folk, attention they learned. Ah, that is how I found my balance. I guess I am part *air folk* too. Water taught them to watch and see, to take care and let be. That I am learning still, I see.

The Sylphs were granted many gifts – and one that none other had. Whatever they imagined, well, they could sing it so. It was they who taught us the power to be still.

In their clever minds they knew the longing of the dragons' hearts: to see lots about them, to know what they did not. So with the lonely dragons they thought, and quickly imagined what to do.

Salamanders, Undines and Sylphs gathered where dragons sit. Well, the fire flits could not sit, and fled away. The Undines flowed after, trying to gather them back. Yet sparks are even quicker than futterblys. They didn't have a chance. The dragons watched and wept.

Suddenly, the Sylphs had a plan. Regardless of what the others did, there the mountains sit. Earth is ever still. What if company for the dragons could be made from the earth?

Once the dragons had saved Earth, and she remembered that. Perhaps then, she would like to make companions for them? Yes, the dragons liked that idea.

To each new creature, Salamander, Undine and Sylph would award a gift: a tiny piece of themselves forever to be held. From fire folk the ability to dance, from water folk the charm to make more, from air folk the talent to speak, those they'd each bestow. Dragons a jewel, a token from the land that made them, to each new form they'd gift as well. Earth did not need to grant a special gift. From Her, each new form became physical, you see.

A healing spirit for each new clan, in safety, the dragon's tokens held. Their jewels were tonics too, for all that needed a cure. By their gems the dragons wish all to see, that of both spirit and earth each creature shall forever be.

CHAPTER 5

Everyone rejoiced. Then out of the mountains came the earth folk. "What have you all decided to do? It is our land too."

Sylphs and Undines, dragons too, looked to sturdy Gnomes, emerging from their earthen homes.

Addressing the dragons first they spoke: "Your longing called us to be, to mine, to tunnel, to carve your jewels. Have you forgotten the offerings we made for you?"

The dragons blushed. The Thunders made them wise, but wisdom always comes later than we'd like.

"We never knew. You never showed yourselves, never spoke. How were we to know?" the first dragon said. The air and water folk agreed. The fire folk were off dancing, so I doubt they even heard.

"Did you never look about you to see?" a young Gnome asked of dragon kind.

There was rumbling amongst the earth lot. Whips of smoke rose from the dragon herd.

A young Sylph approached, her head bowed. "Pardon our folly, gentle earth folk. You are right. We were lost in our sorrows, swept up in our triumphs. Forgive us; that we did not see. Will you join us now?" she asked, very diplomatically (that word means sweet and careful too).

The earth folk grumbled, then laughed. Of course they would help. After all, everything was for beauty and balance to be brought. The dragons sighed. All they'd wanted to do was make a stew.

I guess things are more complicated than we think. I was too shy to contradict, yet thought the dragons had made an excellent stew. Not to eat you see, but to have us all come to be. Dragon stew is not a dish. It's a metaphor; it's not what it seems.

I make metaphors when something reminds me of something else. All the new kin frolicking about the dragons reminds me of all the goodies floating in a stew, a giant Creation Stew. There were winged ones, and crawly things, four legs and magick beings – the ones people call Merfolk and Fae, Elf and Dwarf – oh, and Wizard too. But that is another story. I shall tell it too, yet let me not get confused. Let me tell you first of my kin, the bears.

All the Elementals made companions to dwell in dragon land, all except the Salamanders and Gnomes. That Yorkshire's father told. His father told him. It is a sacred tale that all dragons tell. Anyway, fire couldn't stop to fuss.

Why did fire need form? Water had chosen every imaginable one – from whale to seahorse, droplet to torrent, river, fish, dew and dolphin too. Water beings were sprites, merfolk, sea shrubs (algae), selkies – who knows what else. Fire remained what it was: flame, spark, inspired thought or lightning flash. Salamanders need no herald to be recognized.

Quite opposite are air folk. Being invisible, any shape they could use. That is why some felt there really aren't any air folk.

"Hold your breath and you will see," a Sylph quipped to me.

Their preference was for beauty, and unlike the others on two legs they chose to walk. There were even some that chose to fly.

Balanced and refined, of clear skin and bright eye, quick wit and nimble hand, though rarely seen, even people kind knew of them. They were 'Elfin folk' or 'Fae'. Their enchantments were 'fay-erie'. Stories of their enchantments the people folk called *'fairy tales'*. I'm telling you a fairy tale now. Friends of the wizards; it was for them that the Fae made people kind. Yes, I'll tell you when. Though first of my kind you must hear.

The earth folk, called Gnomes, were quite content to be alone. Inside their mountains they had a fine home. No running about in sun or rain when sparkles could be sought in endless dark. They weren't nasty folk, you see, they just knew how they liked to be.

The dragons wished to bring the land more playful ones. The Gnomes didn't visit or chat; and dragons love to show what they know. They appealed to the Earth, to the great mountains to bring them a companion of strength and cheer.

Across from the dragons, the mountains moved and shook, lightning struck and a huge new shape appeared. It was Great Mother Bear. On her hind legs she stood and bellowed "hello" to the dragons.

She twitched fluffy ears and thick brown fur covered the mountain she had been. She walked on two legs and uncovered boulders, lifting out her cubs. Then all three stood in salute to dragon kind.

So in awe were the dragons, they asked her to guard the sacred jewels and carry the medicine for all the other beings. It would be kept safe by her strength. That she agreed, and to this day in all lands, it is said that only bears hold the medicines of old. That is true, for I have seen them, and carry them too.

CHAPTER 6

How I came to be a bearer of medicine is a tale that will explain all the others I've promised to tell. For you see, they all interweave. Let us begin.

Yorkshire and I were resting from a game of tag.

It was an autumn afternoon. The sky was clear. A wind rose from the east. A party of fairies came into the glen. Yorkshire and I hid.

It was not that we did not like the Elf folk. They were wondrous, clever quick and made beautiful music. No, these were 'Callers'. What is a Caller, you ask me?

Oh, well, you see – that I only sort of knew, then. They are what you call 'legend'. I'd hoped the legend wasn't true.

My mother said the earth was bigger than our little wood. It was hard to imagine what I could not see. Yet I knew my mother'd never tell me what couldn't be.

She said not always do good things happen. Sometimes we cannot see the good in the baddest of times, the baddest of beings. I did not know that Salamanders, Undines, Sylphs, or Gnomes were ever bad, or squirrels, or ravens, or tree folk or anything really. I started to worry. What was this 'bad'?

"Only a word, Little Bear. A word that means there is pain hiding. Cure the pain and bad turns good. All bears know to cure the pain," my mother promised me.

Yorkshire's father taught me why. Bears were made to cure the dragon's pain, to bring their loneliness cheer. I like bringing cheer. But it is also our task to repair. That is why from the Callers I hid. I'm not old enough to be a big bear yet.

I suppose I should tell you what my father told me. The Callers are a special group of Fae. How they are chosen I do not know. Once they are, they are never the same. No longer do they play with Elf, or bears, or dragon kind. They become bearers of dangerous news, ferry warnings or tell of ill fortunes that could change us all. Most dread the sight of Callers.

For us, all is changing. Whatever should occur, we will adjust. The Callers prepare us. Sometimes though, their warnings do not come soon enough. Not all decisions can be made. This was such a day.

Little Dragon and I did not know that. We only knew that Callers brought bad news, so we would have to go home. We did not want to go home. We wanted to play 'pretend'. I was to be a dragon and Yorkshire a bear. I was to make fire.

We sank real low, flat against the ground. The bushes were above us. The Callers came toward us. We held our breaths.

"Friends of the wood hear us. The men folk are attacking dragon kind."

Our eyes got big. Yorkshire started to rise. I put my paw on his claw.

"Friends of the wood hear us. The men folk are attacking dragon kind," the group sang out and passed us by.

"Little Dragon, Little Bear, it is not safe for you to be here. Return to your home," a Caller said from behind us. How did he get there? We did not know.

"Why are people kind hurting dragon kind?" I asked him.

"For jewels and metals and what they have not – all that sparkles in the dark," the Caller replied.

"Those are the earth folks' treasures. I am confused," I said.

"Go home, Little Bear. These things are not for you to change," the Caller said. He patted me between my ears.

"Then what of me?" Yorkshire asked.

"You, Little Dragon, must do what your kind has chosen, to go and never be seen again. Many dragons have died, so have many men folk. Return to your home," the Caller was gone.

Yorkshire and I looked to one another. "No" is what we both said. I did not want Yorkshire to go, never to see him again. I did not want to be surrounded by greedy people folk. Yorkshire did not want to 'pretend' not to be. For as you know, if long enough you pretend, that is what you become.

We knew our parents would worry. Still, we had to see what we could do. We found a raven. We sent her to tell our parents we were safe, and had gone off to find wizard kind.

"Be careful, young ones. Tell wizard kind the raven folk will carry whatever messages they require to still this war 'twixt men and dragon kind."

We agreed.

CHAPTER 7

Yorkshire and I met a wizard once. A frog told us where he lived. We'd heard many tales of wizards. Some were not so nice. Now that I am older I see our parents told us those tales to make us mind. I think you call them 'tales of bogeymen'.

Still wizards are a real and powerful kind, not to be trifled with. It is true, even though now their blood so hides in people kind that their powers are mist. That too happened to Elf kind. You see, Wizards and Elves are related kin.

It was a wizard who taught me that was so, the same wizard whom Frog had sent us to. It was that wizard we sought to find, for he was not mean. He felt sorry for people kind.

He'd be hard to find, especially if he'd heard the Callers. Who knows, he may have sent the Callers. He lived in the most amazing house. Sometimes you could see it, sometimes not. Father said even wizard villages were like that.

His home was all carved and spired, bannered and bright. Then, in a blink, it was just forest land. Well, forest land that was slightly dark and twinkly too. Wizard's homes could be very hard to see, you see. We had to pay attention.

After balance, attention was my most important lesson. Maybe I should put it first. Since when I pay attention, my balance I never lose. Attention, the wizard showed, keeps the pain of falling away.

I liked the wizard. He explained all sorts of things, like what was beyond our wood. I learned of other four-legs in other woods, other winged ones, crawlies and people things. I'd never seen a people thing. I really didn't want to. I heard they killed bears.

The wizard told me not to worry. I was too small to scare the people folk, so they'd not harm me. I asked the wizard what they were, and why everyone feared them.

Yorkshire wondered too. His mother told him to hide from people kind.

The wizard sighed and looked for a moment like he might cry. We feared we'd been impolite. Yorkshire bit his tail and smoke rings came out his nose. The wizard laughed.

"Little friends, people kind are our mistake, we made them incomplete."

I did not know that word. "What is that?" I asked.

"It means something's missing," the wizard answered. That still made no sense to us.

"Oh, it was long ago. Like the dragons, wizards too were lonely once. Most like us were Elf kind, so with them we met. The dragons had gifted all with jewels, with medicines to heal. So we would have to invent gifts for our companion kin. If, of course, we chose to make companion folk."

Yorkshire and I shook our heads. Only the Ancient Ones make other folk. Was this plan of Elf and Wizard a good thing? The wizard shrugged.

"We thought. We took time. The air folk helped. Quick wit and grace they gave, fine form and skillful hand. Yet those were only fleeting. The permanence of all things was already given. We could only grant glimpses of the gifts other folk already held.

"Not all would have quick wit, or fine form, or even skillful hand. Those that did would be blessed but shortly. Their gifts would breeze in, swirl and vanish. You see, it was the fire folk who bore them – and on fire folk none can truly depend.

"Our new creatures could sing and dance, speak and think, love and dream, but only for a time. Unlike Wizard, Elf or Elemental kind they would fade away. They would live and long and then be gone."

"How very sad they must have been, to know elf and wizard and have to leave them behind," I said.

"Yes, Little Bear, that's how our mistake was made. When the Sylph Court conjured them from the earthen realm, the Undine Queens blessed them to create. Like dragons and bears, more of themselves they could make," the wizard said.

"Wouldn't that make them happy?" Yorkshire asked.

"Yes, Little Dragon, it did. It also made them something we had not thought. It made them jealous," the wizard answered.

"Of what?" I asked.

"Of whom, Little Bear. It made them jealous of Elf, of Gnome, of Wizard and Water Sprite, of Salamander and even of your kind – the four legs, winged ones, those that crawl and swim and of dragons too, who guard fabled jewels. You all possess precious things far beyond their means," the wizard said.

"If they can not have them, why do they want them?" Yorkshire asked.

We were both more confused than before. The wizard told us more than we'd imagined. Why did I keep asking?

"They want because they want, dear little friends. Haven't you ever wanted?" the wizard asked.

"More dessert," I admitted. "But it might just make me sick. I do not want what will hurt me," I added. Yorkshire agreed.

"We do not always know what will hurt us. The people thought never dying would be good for them. They strove to achieve it, thinking it had been taken from them – hidden like some treasure. People kind forgot they wanted life. They thought they needed power."

We were spellbound. Mother told me power could not be bought, or borrowed, made or stolen. It was gifted by the Thunders to flow from dragon's breath into all created kind way back in the beginning times. The wizard continued.

"People have no power. They were made without the dragon's gift. They are bits of us, no more, no less. No magick dwells in man, only what slides through them from us. They were made in our reflection, not gifted with one of their own. That is why they long for us, wish to be us, and some even hope to destroy us."

Our eyes got very big. I didn't want to ever leave my wood.

"Like the dragons and the wizards before them, it is only being alone they wish to banish. For deep in their hearts, little ones, it is only we they find." The wizard hung his head.

"How do we fix them?" I asked.

"We can't," he answered. That was the last we spoke of people kind, though we visited the wizard many more times. Never again would he speak to us of people kind.

Now they were killing dragon kind. We had to fix them. If we didn't, our world would vanish. I didn't know where I'd go, where my dragon friend would go. We had to find the wizard again. We had to stop this.

CHAPTER 8

No one would help us. They wanted to flee. The stories we heard multiplied a hundred fold. I knew my mother was worried. I hoped she wasn't crying. I hoped my father wasn't looking for us. Yorkshire hoped his parents were alive.

As we passed through different glens, all were desperate to leave. The magpies scolded us. The futterblys begged us to join them. Then we saw the unicorns.

Their eyes were like starlight, their horns mother-of-pearl in moonlight. I recall how bright they were when my mother once took me to visit. These before us were ashen. One walked over.

"Children, where are your families?" she asked. "Are you alone?"

"We are together," I answered.

"To seek a wizard," Yorkshire added.

"You are very brave. Still you have not answered. Where are your families?"

"We do not know – we hope they live. We can't go back," Yorkshire answered.

"We must find the wizard," I repeated.

"I see. Then know all wizards, Elves, bears, eagles, unicorns, Dwarves, dragons, butterflies, ravens, Wood and Water Sprites, Tree beings, flower Fae, owls, rabbits, elk, Air Wisps – all our folk, everyone is gone to Council. There, I hope, are your families too. Would you like to join mine? We are going there," she said with a gentleness only unicorns possess.

"Thank you, my lady. We would be honored," I said, wanting to sound very well brought-up. You see, even though my mother was not there I wouldn't want to embarrass her, or Yorkshire's.

"Have you eaten? Are you hungry?" she asked us.

"No and yes, my lady," I answered.

"Follow me." She walked towards the group.

Yorkshire nudged me and whispered, "What do unicorns eat?"

"They're vegetarians," I whispered back.

"Thought so," Yorkshire replied.

"Actually, little bear, we do not eat. Still, we feed our guests whatever their hearts' desire. What do you desire, little friends?" she asked so sweetly we felt silly.

"I love pudding and berries, my lady," I answered. Yorkshire looked to the ground.

The unicorn bent over him, almost touching her horn to his head. "Haunch of venison – flamed – and forest mushrooms – I should think," she whispered and her eyes smiled.

Yorkshire looked up and flapped his wings. "Oh yes, my lady – my favorite.

Thank you, my lady," he almost squeaked.

The unicorn and I laughed. "Never be ashamed of what sustains you little dragon, and never forget to give it thanks."

She touched her horn to the ground. A fine linen cloth spread before us. Hot, flamed venison haunch, laden with mushrooms, dripping with juices was set on a silver platter before Yorkshire. I thought his eyes would pop.

She touched her horn to my paw and a silver bowl overflowing with pudding and alpine strawberries appeared.

We were speechless, happy, silly – wow! Nothing like this had ever happened to us.

She moved her horn in an arc above our heads. All sorts of Sprites appeared. "These will serve you. I will leave you to eat. If you need me send a Messenger Sprite. They wear harlequin hats," she said. She went to join her waiting family.

Yorkshire and I feasted. Whatever we thought of, the air folk brought. We tried to speak to them; they did not answer. They were too intent on tending us. We guessed the unicorn arranged it so.

I was quite content. Then I thought. What were my parents doing? Had they gone to the Council? Were they in danger, waiting for me? I should go back. Yet I couldn't desert Yorkshire – and we had to find the wizard.

If the worst happened he'd be our best hope. Yes, I was doing right. I had to go on.

I missed my mother. I wished my father was there to hold me. Then I thought of Yorkshire. He might not have parents at all.

"I hope we find the wizard," Yorkshire suddenly said. His voice was very sad.

"The unicorn will help us; I know she will." I tried to comfort him.

How did everything go so awful? We were just playing when the Callers came. It was going to be pretend. I was going to be a dragon and Yorkshire a bear. Now they wanted *us* to be pretend. We're real, don't they know? Why is everyone else so willing to go?

I was confused. Who were these monster people folk? Were they worse than trolls? Maybe the trolls could eat them. I didn't know any trolls.

Yorkshire and I didn't really sleep that night. The unicorn made us a lovely bed with soft hay. I saw one of my futterbly friends. She looked lost.

"Little Bear, why are you here? Your mother sent us to find you. She is at the Council with your father. I'm lost, so I'm lucky you're not," she said fluttering about my head.

I laughed. "No, I'm lost too. The unicorns are taking us to the Council. We're looking for a wizard."

"The wizards are with the Elf folk, awaiting. Where and what I cannot say. The dragons went far into the north," she said.

"Are my parents there?' Yorkshire asked.

"I don't know. In all the ice and snow I cannot go." She did a back flip in the air. Futterblys, you see, are much daffier than you or me.

Hum, fire and water she said, like in the dragon days, I thought aloud.

"What?" Yorkshire asked.

"When dragons were born – fire and water," I said.

"So?" he asked.

"I don't know; I just thought of long ago, before a mess it all became."

Yorkshire flopped onto his belly, rolled onto his back, let out a little green flame. Then he played dead.

"What are you doing?" I asked.

"Practicing," he answered.

"Stop it. We're going to be fine. We're going to find the wizard and cast a spell and fix it all. You'll see," I said, confidently.

"Good night, Little Bear," he said.

"Good night, Little Dragon. I looked up into the sky and asked the star folk to find my mother and kiss her for me. Star folk will do that, you see, though they will keep secret the kiss was from me.

CHAPTER 9

I like secrets. They're how I keep balance, you see. I know I'm loved and I love me. So it never matters if I fall down; I'll get back up again. That's the biggest secret of all, I see.

Of that I had to keep aware. I was awfully scared. I didn't know what was happening, or what would. For all I knew, we were the wards of unicorns.

Not that unicorns aren't very, very nice. They're just not bears, you see.

"Or dragons either," Yorkshire said. He must have heard my thoughts.

"What are we to do?" I asked him.

"Find a wizard. Get a good scolding. Maybe both," he said.

"You're cheerful," I replied.

"Got to be. How I am won't change what is. Best if we have fun instead. What should we get the wizard to do?" Yorkshire asked, most earnestly.

"I'm not paying attention, huh? I'm spinning on and on. I'm sorry, Yorkshire. Sometimes I'm silly, it's true."

"Which makes me happy. You worry for two. I don't have to. Thank you, Little Bear." He took off flying and did a back-flip.

"Bet you didn't know a dragon could do that, did you? Me neither. Good thing I didn't crash, huh?"

I laughed, imagining a dragon landing like an albatross.

He sat down next to me and held his tail. "Now, tell me what you want the wizard to do?" His eyes got small.

"Well, I thought I knew. You've shown me, I'm rushing to do without a clue. Let's uncover what is. Men folk have gone all mean. Our parents are at Council. Let's go listen, and plan what to do. I don't want the wizard to think me a silly bear, you see." My eyes got very small.

"Excellent. Meantime, let's go play with the unicorns. They know all sorts of games," he said walking towards their camp.

"Wait - we weren't invited." I pulled his tail to protest.

"Of course we were. We're here. We're practically family, silly bear." He walked on. I let go of his tail and followed.

He was right again. Unicorns have the most delightful games. They're magickal, you see. Well, so are we but never mind, let me teach you a game.

It's a lot like hide and seek, though much more wondrous, I think. In it you have teams, certain hide while others seek. When the seekers find the hiders, they switch sides. That is done as quickly as possible, you see.

Now, since unicorns can also shape-shift, they can become hiders you think are seekers. What never changes is the color of their eyes. To keep it all straight, you learn to recognize others just by their eyes.

You look deep to see just what sort they're meant to be. It sounds confused but it's lots of fun. You need be quick, aware and able to pretend. I finally got to be a dragon, and Yorkshire a bear. We were caught by unicorns who'd turned into Faes.

Then we became ourselves and caught the Faes who'd turned into *futterblys.*

Have I confused you again? Unicorns and Fae are 'that' not 'who', you say.

I beg your pardon, and must insist. Beings with spirit are 'he' or 'she', not 'it'. Please say 'who' not 'that' when speaking of me, or Fae or any special ones, I pray. We are neither less nor more than people kind.

Anyway, unicorn hide and seek was tiring, I admit. We lay in the grass, all spun about. After a while we couldn't remember if hiders or seekers we were meant to be.

We laughed a lot and caught ourselves. I guess that's the point of unicorn hide and seek.

We slept well. I stopped worrying. The star folk twinkled and I dreamt. I was eating blackberry pie in my mother's kitchen. The wizard had sent it home with me.

I could just see the wizard. He was speaking. His eyes sparkled like the stars. A map stretched on the table before him. Near his shoulder a white owl perched, studying the map. The wizard was talking to the owl. I wish I knew what he was saying.

I woke with a start. The unicorn stood above me. It was still night time.

"Little Bear, you must know what will be. The Council will decide our time is done. Dragon, unicorn, Mermaid, Gnome, flower Fae and Water Sprite – all will go. Creatures that now speak and sing, dance and dream will be mute. People will come to rule, an empty, hollow land. That is why we are ashen – we mourn what will be," she said to me.

I rubbed my eyes and wanted to cry. No water would come. There had to be another way. I had seen too much to let it pass away. Why should our time be done? Surely not all the land had become a battleground.

"No child, it has not," she said reading my thoughts. "Yet the land will always show what was. In years to come the wise among men will read signs and know what they mean, carved in mountain stone. Here were dragons; there were Gnomes. Go home, my sweet friend – forget what you've seen. Live in your wood, hide from people kind and teach your kin of magick things. Goodbye, little one." She vanished.

Surely that was a nightmare. I couldn't let Yorkshire die; let the silly Sprites go. Little Dragon was my best and only friend. Next morning the unicorn never let on she spoke to me. I was sure I'd dreamt the whole event.

That was very hard on me. I didn't want to think so much. I was just a little bear, you see. I was upset and spun about. Everyone was hurting. There was nothing I could do.

CHAPTER 10

That day we marched through rocky ground and stinky marshes too. Up hills, down dales, across streams and into caves where we sheltered. I was exhausted. My stomach hurt. Yorkshire got a thorn in his claw. We didn't feel so heroic now.

The lands were quiet and still. All our folk had fled. Maybe our quest was not such a good idea. The unicorn and her family walked on.

We climbed a chain of mountains where a dragon fight had been. Everything was charred. No soil was left, just broken, twisted mountain bones. Dragons, horses and men – or what we thought was them – lay aground. I cried.

Yorkshire burnt the corpses of his kin and those of the kind horse folk who were forced to die there too. The smell was horrible; my stomach was worse. To this day you can see images of horse folk white on the hillsides where they fell, and bare, burnt mountain stone that speaks of dragons in a tongue few know.

We walked and walked and found a meadow for the night. The stars shimmered and I wept. How could I fix this mess?

At dawn we arrived. I'd never seen so many kinds of folk. Grand pavilions housed many, great hay beds even more. The air felt prickly – all were unsure. I felt for them, and they for me. Never before have I been happy and sad to be.

At the Great Council I learnt many things. While we searched for the wizard, all sorts of history we heard. When the Elves made people for

Wizard kind, perfect companions they were. They knew us all and with them we spoke. Then they learnt the dragons had made us each a special gift – a precious jewel, a medicine. Well, no such prize was given people kind.

Some were angry, some were hurt, some just thought there are different ways for different folk. Those choices, their descendants bear.

The third kind, who accepted, continued to learn. We taught them about our gifts, that they might heal too. Some married wizard folk, others Elves, and still their descendents carry in them the magicks of old.

The second sort, who were hurt, could not understand. Like me, they did too much spinning and got out of hand. The pain they felt burned like longing. They longed to be gifted folk too – like us, you see. They had no idea they'd been gifted even more than we. They had no special jewel, no single medicine, but a grant to use them all. That I think was better, you see. It told the people folk how much they were loved by those like Yorkshire and me.

The first lot, those who were angry, became very mean. Thinking they'd been denied they turned to destroy. They were the ones who first attacked dragon kind. The second sort supported them.

Those two sought our jewels, for in those jewels they believed was power. Power would gift them as we had been. So silly they were. Yet they made us hurt.

Because of their meanness the Council was called. I've heard it told, wizard folk wanted people folk destroyed. That is not so. People kind were a gift from Elf kind to Wizard kind. In our world a gift cannot be given back.

No, either us or they must change, a new magick worked – else wise all we'd built and known, played and shown, would forever pass away. That, my elders told.

Now I know all I've just said - I was truly scared! I began to imagine, at last, what it is I wanted the wizard to do. I took Yorkshire aside.

"We must speak to the Council," I said.

"Right. A bear cub and dragon imp have wisdom our elders need hear. I think not, Little Bear," Yorkshire said.

"Of course we do. We remember how good it is to play. This is not as serious as they think," I argued.

"Little Bear, you are my friend. Anything, for you, I will do. Still it is true, many dragons have died. My parents may be dead. To me, that is very serious indeed."

"I agree. To let it continue is worse. I think the unicorns showed us what to do.

Remember their game of hide and seek?"

"Sure," Yorkshire said.

I took a deep breath, to say it all before I forgot. "Men seek dragons, and bears,

elves, eagles, air folk, dwarves, fire folk, wizards, too – everyone, anyone they think has more than they. They seek not to learn; they seek to destroy. What if we become something else, something they'd not bother to destroy?" I asked.

"Isn't that what our elders want to do, by disappearing? We've had our time, perhaps now is for people kind," Yorkshire answered.

"I've not had my time, nor you yours. Who are they to seize our time? No. I say we pretend, just as you taught me, just as the unicorns taught us. We must not vanish – where would we go – we must only appear to disappear – pretend. We're hiders, people folk are seekers. Don't you see?"

"No. We're either here or we're not. What are you talking about?" Yorkshire asked.

"I'm not entirely sure. That's what I need to find the wizard for. We must all learn to pretend. Then all the people folk seek is air. We'll no longer be. That's what they'll think. Don't you see?" I asked.

"I don't. Maybe the wizard will. We'll need to sneak past the Elves. It won't be easy. Think the unicorns could change us into Elves?"

"I doubt even a unicorn could do that," I admitted.

"Well, they better. No fat little dragon is getting past a line of Elfin Royal Guard – not even one who can pretend he's a bear," Yorkshire declared.

"Well then, why not get past them as what we are? What harm can little ones do? We're, um - exploring – no, we have a gift – no, news – no …" I was stumped.

"We were adopted, and we've arrived! The wizard adopted us when we lost our families. We're orphans, going to our guardian. That's what we'll say."

"Yes, that does sound good. Let's go," I said.

"No. In the day, we go in daylight, bold as you please. Night looks suspicious, sneaky. In the day we've nothing to hide - it's busy. The elves have more to tend to than strolling orphans. Do you remember his name – the wizard's name?" he asked.

My mind went blank. Every famous wizard I'd ever heard of flashed before me.

Then – Galendryn – yes; that was him. "He was called Galendryn. We just called him Uncle," I said.

"Let's go find the ravens. See if they know where he's camped."

"Silly dragon, he's in the pavilion with the other wizards," I said.

"Nope, that's where we think he is. He wasn't too fond of other wizards. He'd be with his friends, the elves, dragons or bears – or maybe somewhere else. Let's send the ravens," Yorkshire insisted.

"Tomorrow?" I asked.

"No, now. Finding a wizard's night work, right?"

"Then we ask the owls; the ravens are asleep," I said.

"Right, off to the owls. Where are they?" he asked.

I laughed. "Around, I guess. We'll have to look for them."

Off we went.

CHAPTER 11

It was the owls who looked for us. The futterblys told the frogs, who told the forest, so the owls heard we were looking for a wizard. One owl told Galendryn and he sent her to fetch us. She was a lovely snowy owl with blue eyes. I called her Bluebell.

Bluebell flew up behind us, when we thought we were being sneaky. "Who – who" we heard and practically jumped from our skins. We looked up; there she was.

"Are you still looking for the wizard?" she asked us.

"How would you know?" Yorkshire snapped.

"I know what every wizard knows," Bluebell blinked.

"Then the wizard knows we're looking for him?" I asked.

"He sent me to bring you to him," she answered.

"How do we know that?" Yorkshire asked, still miffed.

"You don't, little dragon. You must look into my eyes to see if you trust me," she said. Then she flew off.

I followed, so did Yorkshire.

"It could be a trap," he said.

"By whom? No one cares we're here. No one knows we're here."

"Clearly someone does," he answered.

"The wizard. Please, stop worrying. You're becoming like me," I teased.

"Shouldn't we tell the unicorns? It's rude to disappear," Yorkshire said.

"The unicorns already know."
On we went, following Bluebell's moonlit wings.

CHAPTER 12

"Well, you two have certainly traveled far." It was the wizard's voice. Suddenly we were in his library, yet I knew we'd just been following Bluebell. Wizards are special that way.

I was so happy to see him I nearly knocked him down. Little Dragon flapped his wings and let out blue, yellow, green and red flames. He also jumped up and down.

"I found you. I found you!" was all I could say. The wizard just chuckled and hugged me tight. "My dear little friends, how you two have grown! Shall we have some cookies?" he asked. We nodded.

"Slipping past the Callers was very naughty – and brave too," he said petting Yorkshire's head. "It isn't often I've sent a unicorn, then an owl, to find a bear and dragon."

"Why aren't you with the other wizards?" I asked, as we sat at table. The wizard sighed. Yorkshire blew smoke rings, making Galendryn smile.

"Little friends, I don't agree with what I see. There's too much renegade in me. Men are not the problem. We made them to be. It is wrong to desert them, to just let them be. They will never learn if we refuse to teach."

"Aren't they killing us though?" Yorkshire asked. "What are we supposed to do?"

"Dear little dragon, they can never kill us all. We're far too clever. They're far too dull. We can live in places they can only dream," he answered.

"Then why are we running away? Ceasing to be?" I asked, still quite confused, you see.

"That, Little Bear, is where I disagree. It is our time to help, not hide. Yet the Council does not agree. Elemental kind, dragons, bears, unicorns, Dwarves and Elves, griffins, manticore, phoenix, selkies – most wizards too – have gone another way. They believe our time is done. Earth we should give away. Into our worlds we must retreat – so that never again our blood will be spilt by men."

"What of others like me, the crawlies, the wing bearers, those of fin – well, what of them?" I wanted to know.

"They will go or they will stay. It is for each to choose, his or her own way. Yet none again may ever speak with men. There I also disagree, for what wisdom can men have if it does not come from us who still see?" Galendryn asked.

"Sounds like we've cursed them to me," Yorkshire said, bluntly.

"Ah – it was not called a curse. The Sylph Court called it a charm. The Charm of Unmaking – unmaking the threat of men. You two know that deep inside Dwarf Lair lies Dragonstone - the perfect mother jewel, from which all others come?"

We nodded.

"Made of dragon fire and Gnome bone, She is all colors yet none. Shining bright as the sun, She holds the power to reflect any harm, grant any heal. All that makes gems precious, comes from Dragonstone," the wizard taught.

"The Sylph Lords asked the Gnome Lords to carve a chalice, a great grail, from Her. The Queens of Undine poured living waters inside. We wizards charged that chalice to undo the harm to all, caused by the jealousy of so few. Our spell became known as the Charm of Unmaking.

"In the presence of the Great Council, the Grail Cup was brought, first to the dragons. The first dragon breathed on its waters. The gift of sight was so removed, for all but those with hearts as pure as Dragonstone," Galendryn said.

By the time I became an elder bear, people folk misunderstood that, saying t'was fairy glamour that gave the sight. No, fairy glamour removed the sight. It was fairy glamour that charged the Dragonstone, you see. Let me not interrupt, the wizard was still speaking.

"Second, the Elf rulers received the Sacred Cup. They spoke a silent spell, lifting all knowledge they had brought, except in those whose hearts could love. Therein alone would rest the memory of all the Elves once told," Galendryn said.

In later times I saw that memory spread, told first by poets and bards, then knights of men sought our Dragonstone. They called it Holy Grail. They quested to undo the change we wrought, yet that can only be if men change themselves first, you see. Our Grail hid from them just as surely as did we. Oops, I've interrupted again.

"Third, before Great Mother Bear our Chalice came. Because she safeguarded all our medicines, on all's behalf she acted now. A tear flowed, for what she'd decide. No longer could people kind understand other kind. All medicines, on their own, they'd have to find. None they'd hurt were bound to help, not ever again," the wizard said.

You see, when people folk our elders made, we swore to help them – in honor of Elf and Wizard kind. No more was that to be. People folk, forever on their own now would be.

"Finally, to Horse kind the Cup was brought. Long and humbly they'd served. Often only death was their reward. Forced to help hunt and kill, their hurt now needed air.

"Once we brought you freedom. That freedom shall be a curse 'til, if ever you learn, you too are made to serve," the Horse Lords declared.

"Inside the Sacred Grail Cup our prayers came to life. Henceforth people kind will know our sorrow, thinking it their own. Death, disease, hollowness, fuss – all the nasties brought to us, the Great Chalice turns back to them." Galendryn finished, pouring us more tea.

With the wizard I had to agree. I felt very sorry for people beings. Yorkshire poked me.

"Told you it was a curse. Should we fix it?" Little Dragon asked.

After all, we held magick. Our elders told us so.

"What would you do, little friends? I am happy to listen and be of help," the wizard said. "Me, too," Yorkshire chimed.

I guess I became a big bear then.

CHAPTER 13

"I'm not sure I'm right, you see, but dragons and unicorns taught something to me. Sometimes it is better to pretend than be because then, you see, you are whatever you wish to be.

"I think we should all pretend. We should not go away. We should stay and be what people folk would never expect, you see," I said.

"What's that? I don't want to be a porcupine," Yorkshire complained. The wizard laughed.

"Heavens, no! I think we should help people folk. Help them in ways they can not see," I said, not quite sure what I meant.

"Why encourage 'em? They'll just do it again," Yorkshire said.

I looked to the wizard for help.

"No they won't," he answered. "If I understand Little Bear, he means to change people kind without their knowing. To use the memory the Elves left them – yes, brilliant that is," he said.

I'm glad he knew what I was thinking; I wasn't too sure. I just said what I felt, hoping I'd be a help. "Go on," the wizard said, so on I went.

"I once knew a rabbit, who once knew a girl. She so loved the rabbit she made one of cloth to take wherever she went. All of the rabbit's alertness and care, sweetness and adventure, was put into that cloth.

"At night the little girl held the cloth and dreamt of her rabbit friend. She learned from rabbit kind, grew up and taught her children. I hope still her children's children dream with rabbit kind," I said, and took a breath.

"You want us to be cloth rabbits!" Yorkshire squeaked.

I hid under the table. Galendryn spoke.

"No, he wants us to be dragons, bears, wizards, unicorns, even octopuses too – beloved toys of people kind. Not envied, not hunted, but adored and cherished. Memories made of cloth, held close in dream, to change back the way that people folk see," the wizard explained.

"That is my hope anyway," I said from under the table.

"Come up here, Little Bear. I won't eat you. Being a stuffed dragon beats being a dead dragon anytime," Yorkshire sang.

I came out. "Besides, it's only pretend. The wizard will use our spirits to power the toys, just like the Cup. We'll be free to be where or what we choose – like in unicorn hide and seek. Besides, it was you who said it's rude to disappear," I said, quite sure.

"Right. I've got another idea" Yorkshire said. "One a turtle taught to me. She lived in our cave. Cloth burns; rock won't.

"Once this turtle knew a boy. They went everywhere, exploring. The turtle even taught the boy to swim. Well, one day the boy's mother thought to make turtle soup. So the turtle had to go away; before she left she gave the boy a stone and showed him how to carve. She told him if he carved her picture, with him she'd always stay.

"Guess my stone turtle's like your cloth rabbit, huh? Gifts from friends who can no longer be, yet want their love to always be, see?" Yorkshire asked.

He turned to the wizard, "Can you make stone dragons and bears, and all the others, Galendryn?"

"For you, little dragon, I can do anything," the wizard bowed his head.

We had fixed it! I was so proud.

CHAPTER 14

I couldn't wait to tell my parents. I was a Big Bear now. Yorkshire flapped his wings. Bluebell's stand blew down. She flew to me. Yorkshire was a Big Dragon now – mighty and wise, he winked an eye to Galendryn.

What the wizard did, I can never tell. Suffice it to say all things are magick still. In every corner we do lurk. In stuffed or stone, there we sit. So, if your world wearies you, or things become too mean – remember you are not alone. We did not all run.

Those who wished to go are gone. Yet others of us stayed. You must look to find us, I'm sorry to say. We're here because we love you. We hope you'll love us too. When you do, you'll know what it was came special from the Elves to you.

I am tired of storytelling now, yet wish you not to worry. We found our parents, got lots of hugs, but couldn't go out for weeks. The world sorted itself, as it is known to do.

Long after we'd grown, when we were wise as ever we'd be, Yorkshire and I went off to become toys, just like the ones you see.

We needed new adventures. That was it, you see. Please, for us do not grieve. Yet when you hold a teddy bear or fluffy dragon imp, please remember what we were, even what we did.

For you, we were heroic and though I may confuse, I'll tell you exactly what the wizard told me to. In that long ago you see, what we were, is why you are. Don't ask me to explain. Study Dragonstone and the spells we spun. I'm afraid that's all I'll say.

Oh dear – Yorkshire's asked me something. Yes, in the meantime, won't you come find us? We'll play unicorn hide and seek. We very much look forward to finding you. Would you like to find us too?

Adventures of Bear & Dragon 1
In England, Wales and Paris too

CHAPTER ONE

As told by Little Bear (to his people friend)
Many long years had passed since Yorkshire and I hid, or played, or even saw each other. You see, we both became toys – he a stuffed dragon and I a stuffed bear. No longer could we choose, so separated we became. Alas, even our hopes were gone; it was the age of men.

He was taken off with whom to do what I never did learn. I passed from hand to hand, was loved and lost and loved again. Then one day I was thrown into a garbage bin.

All my hopes for people kind fell with me, far down that chute. I hoped and prayed and hoped again, my dragon or wizard friend would come save me from the stinky mess I was in. Yet there I sat, all tumbled about. No one loved me anymore you see.

How could I have come so far to sit in oil and muck and moldy stuff? What was it I had done? Why was I here? Once I was loved and loved me. Now I felt very hopeless you see.

Just then a lady came into the courtyard with the garbage and me. She stopped and turned and looked. She walked over and knelt, then she spoke to me: "What are you doing there, little bear?"

"They threw me away, you see" I answered, never expecting her to hear. She did!

"Well, only a nut would throw away a teddy bear as fine as you. Come home with me." She picked me from the bin and patted my head. "Don't be afraid little one, I shall take you home."

I felt happy now. She loved me. I could tell.

"First I must bathe you, to wash off the muck. Then I must frankincense you to cleanse away the idiot who threw you out. Then a new bow I think. Yours is all tattered. Would you like that? Oh – what is your name?" she said, then asked of me.

"Little Bear" I said.

"Little Bear, I am me" she said and shook my paw. "What color bow should I get for you?" she asked.

"Sparkly and green" I answered.

"Sparkly and green it shall be, Little Bear. Never fear again. To hurt you they must go through me, and I'm nowhere near as nice as I look" she winked and kissed my nose.

Perhaps she was part wizard kind, perhaps a portion Fay. Long ago I thought their blood had gone away. Yet who was this people kind who knew of secret ways, who spoke with me as plain as any in the olden days? I was confused again and thought I best be silent for a time.

That she did not mind. She held me and fed me, and even asked what were my favorite foods. In winter she wrapped me in her woolen scarf. In summer she bought me a little chemise, made just for me, with suns and moons and shooting stars. She took me to the country and even to graduate school. She had a horse and took me riding too.

She told her friends about me that I could speak, though wasn't "the blathering type". They thought her odd and chuckled that stuffed animals might speak. So when I got a few alone I spoke a word or two. They would scream then she would smile. She had a very different style.

One day she left me home. She said she was leaving graduate school and that I need not see. I remained as silent as cloth can ever be.

When she came home that evening she had a surprise for me. She'd gone into a toy store and found a little dragon that spoke - just like me.

She'd never seen a stuffed dragon, let alone one that insisted she buy it. It told her its name was Yorkshire and that she must take it home. Then it flapped its wings. Afraid that it might fly about the store, she thought it best to take it home.

You can just imagine how big my eyes became. So shocked was I, I could not speak.

"Hi there, Little Bear" Yorkshire said to me. Still I could not speak.

Yorkshire turned to the lady, "He's always been a little shy. What's for dinner? I like mine grilled."

The lady started laughing. "So do I little dragon. Yet I fear the servants are all on strike. Much has changed since you were young, since I was young, so let's just take this slow. You are a stuffed toy now; it is safer for us all if you remember to pretend" she instructed and left the room.

Yorkshire and I looked at one another. We were definitely in the right place. We hugged and laughed and danced about, celebrating almost right off the dresser top. Here we are after all we'd been – we were little again!

Whatever should we do? 'I need some time to be' I heard myself answer to me. Delighted as I was to be with Yorkshire again, I was weary of trying to fix things. My last attempt had sent me to the garbage bin. I wanted to sit and settle and eat dessert. I felt my days as hero just hadn't worked.

Yorkshire thought me silly, but that he always did. Instead I just let the lady hold me and closed my eyes a bit. Yorkshire sat up on his perch, awaiting my return. He still felt we had much to do. I felt we had already been.

This time it was the lady, they called her Christine, who woke me up to go questing again. Very often she reminded me of my old wizard friend, Galendryn. In her world she did not fit. Her kind she did not trust. Like me she was weary. Unlike me she was losing hope.

For her, people beings were mean and one day would destroy all sign we had been. It was just a matter of time. Christine walked in the world like a ghost of what had been.

She, Yorkshire and I lived together for more than twenty years, and I watched her spirit drain. Things she knew, she questioned now. Had it been a dream, or had she woke in a nightmare somehow? I had to help her see. She had for decades protected me, and Yorkshire, and others of our kind. It was simply our turn you see.

I decided to do what I thought I never would – to help the people beings. The Council had forbidden us to speak, especially of the time before the rule of men. Though I was merely stuffed, I knew I was in greater danger now than ever I'd been. Here is why.

This is quite a lot for my foam-filled head to sort, so please bear with me, if you would. When the Charm of Unmaking (see *The Bear & Dragon Tales* for explanation) was wrought, the Council overlooked that elves and wizards had married people kind.

Their children they forgot. So when our knowledge the Elf Lords removed, it made an emptiness like an infection that spread in all with any people blood.

Even those whose ancestors included wizard or Fay were destined to harbor that seeping forgetfulness. Soon I feared only myths and stories would remain, nothing real would resound in our names. To all we would be 'fairy tales' that none would know were fact. I could not let that be.

That's what was happening to my friend you see. The infection was there; she was forgetting. I couldn't just tell her. I needed something more. I was so confused and worried too. I was just a little bear – a stuffed little bear. So much had been left for me to repair.

"And me. Don't forget me. I'll burn 'em up if need be" Yorkshire pledged. I laughed.

"No silly dragon we need repair, yes – remind people kind they were once one with us" I said.

"We can do that too" Yorkshire assured ever confident even when I hadn't a clue.

I loved my dragon friend. His bravery didn't know what hopeless meant. With Yorkshire nothing ever was.

"How would you remind the world of men?" I asked, not really expecting an answer.

"Tell the lady" he said, without even pausing for a breath.

"Tell her what?" I asked.

"A fairy tale silly bear, about us – when you were a bear cub and I a dragon imp. If she understands she may have some ideas too" Yorkshire said, shrugging.

"But she's people kind. Remember the Council – we're forbidden." Yorkshire bit his tail and columns of smoke came out his nostrils.

"If she's people kind, I'm a unicorn. Besides", he continued, "we haven't exactly been stuffed animals these twenty years. Have we?"

"No" I admitted.

"Too late to stand on ceremony then. Better tell her." he insisted.

I was so relieved, in something this important my best friend thought just like me.

CHAPTER TWO

"Good morning guys!" the lady came into our room with coffee and treats. She set me with her in bed. Sometimes she read to us. Sometimes she wrote. Sometimes movies we would watch. She took a sip of coffee.

"Dragons are not real, she said" I said to her.

"What?" she asked.

"Dragons are not real, she said" I repeated.

Yorkshire and she both regarded me. "Excellent opening line, Little Bear. Well, go on" she said to me.

"That's all! Write it down. The rest I'll tell you in the English countryside. Let's go to the English countryside" I said.

Yorkshire looked at me like I'd popped a seam. Christine grinned. "You know, in all the years I've known you I don't think you've ever said so much. Very well, I'll see what I can do. The English countryside, huh? All right, why not? You could have picked the far side of the Himalayas I suppose."

"Too cold" Yorkshire snapped.

"Right; I think I've been letting you both watch too many movies. Too much "Fellowship of the Ring", or maybe it was "Harry Potter".

She laughed, realizing this was her fault. She'd raised us on The Hobbit and The Last Unicorn. We were fans of Mystery Theatre and Sherlock Holmes. The day she'd bought Yorkie she promised to take him to Wales. He remembered.

You see, all dragons come from Wales; it's a necessary pilgrimage – like Muslims to Mecca, Jews to Sinai or Christians to Jerusalem. Dragons must go to Wales.

Definitely the lady had made this be, whether she knew it or not. Soon she bought the plane ticket. We were going home! She had no idea what we were about to do. Neither exactly did we.

"Well little ones, we're going across the sea. We're staying in the countryside, in Shropshire, on the Welsh border. You can tell your story, and Yorkshire, I'll take you into Wales – as I promised I'd do" she announced one day with glee.

We played stuffed animals, most convincingly. We didn't want to let on what we'd done – you shall see. As no doubt you know, the Old World is very different than the New.

It is true we find our focus in the land. Finding our balance is trickier, be you four legs or magick kind. Yet for people beings, balance can only be found when they hold an ancestor's hand. That is why in every land, before their heart they forgot, people kind prayed to those who came before and sought counsel from us.

You see, in the Old World relations stand unbroken to the days when we all spoke. In the New, broken many times their line has been. It is difficult to find them, harder still to know them. Ask around and the truth I am telling, you will see. Why it is I wish I knew, yet sadly it is so. People kind have separated from their ancestors that have been, and from us who sang to them.

In the New World lands it is very hard to hold one's ancestors, harder still for them to hold you. Please do not think nothing that means, for remember how hopeless I felt when no one held me? It is the same for any one you see. America is oft a painful place to be.

Yet silly as it seems, people kind believe they can run alone, live separate from you or me. We see only pain that has brought, for none are the loners they fancy to be. They have closed their hearts, so they won't have to see.

Our task (us non-'s' folk – we who are more than toys) is to open those hearts – slowly – so their eyes may adjust again to see us. Oh dear, I'm in a grand mess indeed. People kind have lost more than he Council ever took.

"Little Bear, why do you look so worried?" Christine suddenly asked, interrupting my fearful thoughts.

"Are you scared of airplanes? You liked them before" she said and showed me a pair of wings I'd been given when we'd ridden a plane.

"Remember how much you could see?" she picked me up to remind me. She hugged me and kissed my head.

I closed my eyes and saw my mother, then Great Mother Bear. I felt strong again, and very old. Bears were made to help in times such as these. Besides, now I had two best friends: a dragon and elfish people being. Who knows together what we might unbind?

CHAPTER THREE

Our plane journey was very long. The sun went down and came up again. Yorkshire thought it was fun. Sometimes it was bumpy; I was scared. Christine covered us in a blanket. We went to sleep.

When we arrived a very official customs kind saw Yorkshire. "British citizen" he declared "and his bear friend too", then he motioned us all 'Go through'.

Christine smiled; Yorkshire flapped his wings. He was awake again. "See Little Bear, I'm home. We'll have fun" he said.

I was happy to be recognized by people beings again. We were petted and talked to and welcomed home. I'd never been in Britain, yet maybe I had.

Why is it in America people kind pretend they don't see us, or we embarrass them? They become nervous, or even mean. Here they smiled on us, and I giggled. On the other side of the sea, mostly stuffed I pretend to be. Here I woke up.

As soon as we arrived an adventure began that took us far past my bedtime. Wrong directions we received after our second plane trip, and through the rain we wandered. First we drove almost to Liverpool (too north), then back around into Wales (too West) where Yorkshire cheered, across to the outskirts of Chester, down motorways, through medieval villages and fairy tale towns that were not on any map you see.

Something hit the wing mirror. It shattered. I jumped; it was dark and hard to see. We were following a person who was leading, rather too quickly, down lanes we'd never seen. We could not stop. I hid in the backpack, near Yorkshire. It stopped raining.

Those we met were kind and tried to help. Problem was we were going where none of them had ever been. So try as they might, we lost our way again. Ten hours it took to find our bearing. We avoided Birmingham (too south), ventured back into Wales (West again), went towards Shrewsbury (north a bit) and finally found our way – east and a little south. I was entirely turned about!

That night we slept in a cozy manor. It was the first bed we'd seen in almost two days. My clock was completely confused. I admit, I longed to go back.

Christine wouldn't hear it. "Little Bear we're on adventure. All great adventures start out hard. Good night."

CHAPTER FOUR

It was to ravens cawing that I awoke. The sun was soft. The sky was pale turquoise – the gardens a mix of emerald, garnet, topaz, peridot – oh, and citrine too. I could see a stone lily pond from our window. I thought of our koi pond in California. Lilies, like white alabaster, were blooming. Flowers of pink tourmaline sparkled like little bells ringing the pond.

It was more peaceful here, I had to admit. All my confusion and worry had dropped off overnight. I watched sprites hop from lily pad to bellflower, disappearing in the sun's light. Goldfish tried to catch them. Silly fish! There were futterblys (butterflies) and black/whites (magpies) too. Horse kind grazed the grassy fields.

In the distance the craggy ridges of the Welsh borderlands spoke 'hello'. I could see where Yorkshire's relatives guarded and flew. There I wanted to go. Here is magick land you see, and I started to remember how it felt when I was still a grizzly cub.

Christine went exploring and tucked us into bed. That she did for about a week. We did not mind. We spoke to ancestors and sprites and magick kind who came everyday to play. From them we learned lots we did not know.

Seems in the not so long ago our friend's people had left this land. Across the sea they went, not intending to remain, so those they would have brought were left to stay. Alone her people went to a place they did not know. Neither did that place of them know. There were no relatives to welcome or protect, for counsel or to remind respect.

Together they lasted in an uneasy way, which you can easily see today. In many ways the land where we were born is an orphanage, you see. I fear for the lost children of people kind. When little dragon and I long ago were lost, wards of unicorns we soon became. From the American Lands, I do believe, the unicorns have all been chased away.

Here in the comfy Shropshire countryside, warm in my bed, I felt a chill, a great sadness creeping up. Seems I was not the only creature who'd been tossed into the garbage bin. For the first time I felt pity for the people kind I'd left across the sea.

"Ah" said Yorkshire, "how do we get them out again – out of the garbage bin?"

"How indeed?" I thought.

One morning our friend packed us into her pack and took us to a large medieval town. Everywhere we looked were remnants that we'd been. It was plain to see why British people folk smile at us (well, all the Europe folk do). They talk to us and give us treats.

Here ancient wood and brick, gargoyles, stone dragons, embroidered unicorn and water sprite, mosaic angels, tapestries with crawly folk, stained glass bright with messenger Fay. All their world declares of us. Everyday it's we they see, peeking from rooftops or down garden lanes, standing on hillsides, peering from turret tops and towers too.

We crown columns, guard bridges and bring needed cheer. How can we be forgotten? We are everywhere.

Not so where we were born. On the other side of the sea few reminders, if any you'll see. No wonder they are so nervous there to speak to Yorkshire or me. They've heard of familiars, but don't believe they be. It's funny sometimes how belief won't let you see.

So we watched our friend with glee. She thought it was she who was leading us you see. No matter, we had her take us where her kin had been. Cafes, cathedrals, village shops, even battlefields where they'd walked. We wished her to hear them again. Remember how important holding an ancestor's hand is for a people being? Meeting a few wizards and Fay would do her good as well. So we pretended to let her lead.

See, her spirit folk had told me to bring her to them. Remember when I asked her to take me to the English countryside? That was the only way we (Yorkshire, me and them) figured to counter what the Elf Lords had wrought. For even magick folk make mistakes, you see. It's then left for bears to find a repair.

"And for dragons to guard them while they do. Though I think we're quite unique" Yorkshire added.

"Well for one thing we're stuffed" I reminded, "and little too".

"With all the knowledge of being big" countered Yorkshire. "We couldn't be more perfect if we'd planned it."

"Who said we didn't? Remember when we chose to become toys? We weren't going on holiday, you know. It was to help the silly people folk." I recalled for us both.

"Right. So what precisely are we going to do?" Yorkshire stared his dragon eyes at me.

"I for one want lunch. Look there's a Bear's Cafe over there" I said.

"This whole country has Bear's inns and pubs and shops and cafes. Never said your family were all tycoons." Yorkshire declared.

"Never knew. I'll buy lunch." I said.

"No, you'll pretend to buy lunch and I'll pretend to eat it" he said.

"Hey guys", Christine interrupted, "Let's go to that Bear's Cafe and eat."

That meant we were going for lunch. We were a good team, the three of us.

CHAPTER FIVE

After lunch we walked across to an old stone church. Christine told us it kept calling to her, though she couldn't imagine why. We played stuffed and went along.

The cool, dusky inside was decorated for Harvest – rather unusual for a church as I saw no crosses. The aisle was garlanded with gourds, wheat and dried flowers. I caught sight of the tiniest of Fay hiding in the offering baskets and swinging playfully on those garlands.

They waved to Yorkshire and me. I waved back; Yorkshire flapped his wings.

Behind the altar glowed a large oval stained glass window (of more recent vintage) depicting the goddess of the harvest overseeing her fields.

Christine told us "Guys, that's the Goddess Demeter – I know, my middle name's for her. Where are we?"

Just then we looked up and glimpsed a dragon spirit climbing into the tower. Where are we indeed? We found a plaque and learnt the church was built in the 10th century by none other than our friend's great, great, great, etc. paternal grandmother. From then on we called it 'grandma's church'.

It was so nice to be in a relative's house. We came there often to write the Tales. In a month we only saw one other person, and not for long. We did learn there was a myth about a dragon in the tower.

They called it the devil, silly folk. They said it climbed into the tower on All Hallows Eve night to survey its' throne – a place on the borderlands called The Devil's Chair. Well, we'd seen a dragon's ghost (a dark blue green worm-type) in clear daylight almost a fortnight before All Hallows Eve.

Yorkshire told quite a different story about 'The Devil's Chair'. It had been a meeting ground and place from which the borderlands could easily be guarded by his kin. The dragon spirit in the tower had done the same for the town, being a sort of relay station for those on the borderlands. Well, that was before the dragon wars, I suppose.

We went down to the river to watch the swans then went journeying all around. See, when we weren't writing we were searching for a place Christine had seen the night we got lost. Of course we were also visiting the countryside – going to ruins.

I learnt something there too. If you go when almost no one else is around, the stones will sing to you, stories you'll here, sometimes events you'll see from long ago when the buildings were new.

I began to wonder why that was so common here but not so across the sea. I had to visit a lot of places, speak to many sprites listen to the ravens and swans, before I began to understand.

In the Old World many things have been protected and preserved. People kind no longer speak with us – for the most part (there are exceptions) – yet we know they care for us. They have not entirely forgotten us.

We are not just the dust of legend or the dewdrops of imagination. We hold up the garden gate, or guard a favorite pub, or inhabit a tree the same family has picnicked under for more than four centuries. We are family, perhaps distant and mute but loved just the same.

How very powerful it is to have someone, anyone care for you – and know they do. It matters not if you be people folk or magick kind, in this we are exactly the same. My spirit felt happy again, not chased away or ignored. It was a bit like growing in a beautiful garden. Yes, here there are lots of gardens.

CHAPTER SIX

We went to a lovely one, in a place called Hodnet. First we went into the village, to a restored rocking horse shop. It was owned by a lady who knew our kind well. There were great carousel horses and little push ones too. There were even teeny versions that tiny sprites might ride.

The shopkeeper allowed me on a push horse, who was very talkative. She told me where she'd come from, and that, just like me, she'd been cast aside you see. I told her we'd have bought her, but she was already sold. I wished her happiness wherever she might go.

Meanwhile Yorkshire chatted with a stuffed elf who sat there to greet folk. Of course they were talking food and the elf recommended the Bear's Inn for lunch. I laughed.

"Better be good" Yorkshire said.

It was. I've not had Atlantic crab before – quite yummy, and I'm more partial to dessert, so it was special indeed.

Afterwards we walked across the road to a churchyard. We kept walking and found our way into the gardens. You could feel them breathe. Here was not a haunted wood, but a place where magick folk roam, where tree spirits live, where undines play – even if they do wait until the tourists have gone away.

Clearly visiting season was over.

Christine didn't mind. "Little Bear if I'm correct these were owned by kin of mine; it's family ground, no one will mind – that's our secret, okay?"

Yorkshire and I agreed. We knew our friend was listening, else wise she would not have gone on. Maybe it was because only caretakers were there, maybe it was because of her, or maybe because of us – whatever caused it, we were spellbound. The air pulsed, the sunshine tingled and everywhere we looked were little folk.

Of different colors, forms and personalities they tended to each flower and stone, running up branches, skipping down lanes, sunbathing on lily pads. Some even seemed more interested in us than we were in them. Others were so focused, probably nothing else they could see. Soon I would learn how wrong I can be.

We found a spot to sit, the bottom of a stone landing overlooking a lake, the pastures beyond and a large part of the gardens. Our friend kept rubbing her eyes, not believing what they were seeing. Yorkshire and I tried not, even silently, to giggle.

Soon she relaxed, for enchanted she became. She watched the air space near a golden leaf birch wiggle. Two air sylphs had collided and a bark gnome, as crusty as his trunk, was raising something of a complaint.

Suddenly there came a loud HONK and up rushed a great black swan. He wasn't angry with us – it was those sylphs he expected better from! Harshly he let them know. But already they'd vanished, all had, leaving us completely alone on the serene, perfectly groomed grounds a split second before he'd arrived, bellowing.

Deprived of his audience he turned to lecture us. We were on his grounds and as long as we stayed on the landing he didn't mind. If we walked onto his lawn, he'd get us, just like those sylphs. Yorkshire and I got very big eyes.

Christine laid back and laughed. "I wonder if this is how Lewis Carroll wrote 'Alice in Wonderland' – in an English garden? What do you think guys?" she asked us.

"I think we're definitely down the rabbit hole" Yorkshire answered.

I laughed. Then we sat for awhile enjoying the autumn sun. That was it really; what made here so unique (and Paris too I'd later see). These gorgeous gardens aren't just for show. Not only do these people folk preserve wood and stone; they preserve places for magick folk to roam. That's what their great gardens are, reserves for us magick folk. Seems endangered species now are we.

"Better endangered than extinct, Little Bear. Any day, I should think." said Yorkshire with a big dragon's spunk.

He was right, of course, you see.

"That's what they're missing across the sea, deliberate places for us to be." Yorkshire concluded.

"You're not suggesting an Act of Congress, are you?" Christine inquired.

We both looked startled. I guess we knew, but then we didn't, our friend had been listening too.

"Let's move" we both said simultaneously.

"Ah, little ones, that is more complicated than you think." she said.

"Did you know, long before I met you, that is precisely what I intended to do? I think I had to meet you both, and there are things we have to do, yet perhaps one day we can all move." she added. I felt we'd made her sad.

"Let's go see where the magick folk went" Yorkshire said. We walked around the gardens and found them all again. It was lovely to see them safe and happy in places of their own.

CHAPTER SEVEN

In the weeks that followed, even when Christine was off somewhere, we'd come back to visit our garden friends. To the rocking horse shop too we would go, especially at night. We rode lots of horses and listened to the stories of elf-kind. Many found their way into the Tales, some did not, you see.

In our nighttime adventures we learned of dragons too. We were told of an old dragon city called York, and promised that Yorkshire had been named for a county where many of his ancestors once reigned. We were told we had to go – and into the Scottish Highlands, too – there is something there for me, the elves promised you see.

So off we went to York. Scotland shall have to wait, for we must also go down to Salisbury, then London, and our time is getting short. But we know we'll all be back, as often as we can, or so we really hope.

We rode the train, which was fun for me; I'd not been on a train before. Well, not this long. We'd taken many a short ride into Wales – to meander about and visit Yorkshire's kin. But I'll get back to that, it will make more sense if first I take you into York.

I mean the old city of course, behind the walls. Never have I seen so many people, spirits and things jostled all together and moving who knows where. I was reminded of San Francisco's Chinatown, except these weren't Asian people folk. So much was going on, I was easily confused.

Yorkshire told me not to worry, he would soon explain. We went to the cathedral, the largest in the Northern Hemisphere, for evensong one night. Yorkshire told me to look up at the nave, that dragon was his mother you see.

I was most astounded; there was a dragon in the nave! There were all sorts of gargoyles in the choir room, making funny faces from their columns. I think they were there to humor the singers during long hours of practice. You will not see them in the rest of the church.

You will see the dragon and several Green Men, angels – perhaps some are Fay – and many beautiful things. I was happy to be there, and we went every night to evensong. I giggled at the gargoyles.

We went into the crypt and the Minster library. Seems the city was founded by the Romans and the dragon was its ancient seal. Today what they call the Yorkshire Dales was dragon land. We could not go to visit though. Trains were no longer running; it was November you see.

In the crypt we got to visit our friend's great, great, etc. grandmother again. We;; sort of. We learned she's really in Notre Dame in Paris you see. Ir was getting complicated for me.

Seems Christine and Yorkshire had a real connection to this land. I did not feel left out. My kin would speak to me at Stonehenge you see.

Yorkshire told me why York's so confusing to me. People folk had camped on dragon land. In the past, and in Viking times, the dragons had been the guardians and overseers of York. After the wars that blessing no longer flowed. It backed upon itself, so did many spirit folk. They trapped themselves, energized though unable to leave.

Many bad and bloody things happened there too. Backing upon themselves, they neither could flow. You can feel them still.

I decided I'd stay in the B&B and asked Yorkshire to accompany me. We met the innkeeper's young nephew. He wanted to take us back to Ireland you see.

Christine had gone to the Minster to study illuminated manuscripts. She went to a shop and bought frankincense oil. She came back and anointed us – to clean away all the mucky stuff. Then we went to the cathedral for evensong and I listened to stories from Yorkshire's mom.

I saw the things she'd done, the places she'd been, I was happy again. Yorkshire had been concerned, I knew. See, he's a green dragon and when we went into Wales everyone teased him. Well, that's because Welsh dragons are red you see – or so they told him and me.

"Since when do people folk know what color dragons are meant to be? In my time they called us Common Welsh Green. Though some fools even thought we had no wings. I loved flying over them!" Yorkshire's mom assured me.

Her scales glimmered in flame. I knew then not only fire but poison she could breathe. I was scared; I meant no offense. I was just a little bear, still you see.

First we'd gone into Wales by car. Before we went Yorkshire was told he was the wrong color to be Welsh. Soon after we crossed the border, we passed "The Green Dragon Inn".

"Must be English" Yorkshire quipped to me, but I knew what he meant to say.

He'd come all the way across the sea (not to mention what he'd done before we became toys) to be told by people kind he just didn't belong in the birthplace of dragon kind. His eyes went yellow and sparks came out his nostrils. I wanted to help, but didn't know how.

The next time we went into Wales, and he fussed all the way, it was on the train. We stopped at a resort town, mostly abandoned as it was November. We went into a deserted Victorian building, built atop what had been a Roman spa. From its rafters hung a large Welsh flag. Its prominent red dragon greeted us with a sparkling eye. Christine left us alone.

The dragon spoke quite clearly – not minding that Yorkshire was green.

"Welcome home, my dear little grandson. Be sure you gather dragon stone, before you cross the sea again. You will know where it will be. Then of course, you must come back to me."

"Wow! She spoke a riddle. I've always heard of dragon riddles. She's your grandma?" I asked Yorkshire very excitedly.

"Well, great, great, great, way long ago, etc. – sure, I suppose. Little Bear – we get to go to a dragon lair! You, me and the lady too – that's the stone she meant. I'll show it to you. We've got to keep our eyes open, hearts too. That's the way to find a real dragon lair." Yorkshire said.

"You mean there are real dragons still?" I asked. My eyes were giant size.

"I don't know – but our enchantment remains. It can be found, in a lair, even collected. Yet nothing it will do unless it was gifted by a dragon to you. Grandma just gifted us." Yorkshire's eyes were emerald now and real giant too.

Just then our friend returned. "That's very cool – to have a giant dragon on your national flag. I wish other countries did stuff like that. I'd be really proud to have a flag like that, wouldn't you?" she asked us.

"Let's move here!" we said in unison.

"Buy us a house." I added.

Christine laughed. "Tell you what, you two get me the gold, I'll buy you the house. I promise." she said.

Yorkshire and I looked at one another, very excitedly. Wow, to have his grandma on our national flag!

"Shall we go up to the lake for tea?" Christine asked.

We were both sidetracked. She smiled and picked our pack up, hoisting us over her shoulder. As we walked out she called back "Bye, grandma" and waved. We didn't say a word.

CHAPTER EIGHT

"You know little ones, there's Welsh blood in me. It's not like we'd be coming to a strange country. This land remembers me." she said, petting our heads.

Then she told the sky not to rain, for it was getting very dismal and almost charcoal gray. At the lake there was no tea, but there were lots of swans. There was a small odds and ends tourist shop that was still open too. We bought some bird seed and Yorkshire asked Christine to buy me a pewter dragon pin. He's wears a silver and turquoise bear charm I gave to him.

"There you go, a real Welsh mountain dragon – for a real Welsh mountain bear" Yorkshire said pinning the dragon charm on my woolen jacket.

I was very proud to wear my friend on me. The lady had given me a silver bear that tinkles and an Evil Eye to wear, years ago. Now I had a dragon too.

We went to feed the swans, and hear their stories of summertime. One came up to us. "Well, well – a young dragon – and green – and a little bear cub. My, my - I know of Marine Blues, Royal Reds, even Silver Ashes of the snowy mountain side, yet the Greens I thought were legend." he said in awe.

"Hey everyone, look over here!" he trumpeted. "The Green Dragon's returned!"

Yorkshire hid in the pack. I'd never seen him be shy before. All the swans on the lake came up to look, and bow their long beautiful necks. Yorkshire peeked out, and they gasped.

Next morning at breakfast the innkeeper remarked, "Oh, mustn't be Welsh. That one's green." Yorkshire decided it was time to leave.

After we settled the account we literally ran to the train station – just in time to – and headed back for Shrewsbury (on the English side). There everyone pet Yorkshire's head and fed him grilled treats – oh, and thought he was Welsh. That's the medieval town with grandma's church and the Bear's Café and we liked it a lot. I like medieval towns, they remember me and Yorkshire too, you see.

On the way back, there was a sudden change in plan – we were on the borderlands, passing a very high, eerie rock formation. Christine got all goose bumpy, my eyes got big.

Little dragon squeaked "Stop. That's it."

Well we couldn't stop; we were on a train. Instead Christine took pictures, thinking that way we could show them and find this place again. There were no signs you see. We'd left a Welsh station, and the next one was English – so our spot was smack on the borderlands. Clearly it was a lookout. We had to go there. It had called us you see.

The lady who owned the manor house where we were staying is Welsh. She knew exactly where we meant and took us on excursion there. We stopped for breakfast at a little village in Wales. It had a garage called 'Elf" and the best scones I've ever seen. They didn't mind that Yorkshire was green, and asked what he'd like to eat.

After a leisurely meal we drove to the mountain's base. It took us quite a while to climb to the top. Christine kept telling us we weigh too much! The view was spectacular.

Here's the real Middle Earth were Bilbo lived. "Bet the Lonely Mountain's in the Yorkshire Dales." Yorkshire said.

"Well, we'll go find out. Look at the creatures in these rocks. Ooo, dragons lived here, for sure. Almost I can smell them." Christine said.

We could. Yorkshire led us off in search of dragon stone. He found a piece and gave it to me. It was very red with green and black and filled with sparkles, like tiny diamond jewels. He found another and gave it to Christine, "For your medicine bag", he said to her.

Then he found a third, "For Uncle Roger, too. When we get back he'll have a stone from our home". he said.

Uncle Roger is a Lakota contrary (like the contrary elves and contrary wizards – those who with the Council's decree did really disagree). He gave Yorkshire a Thunder Spirit charm to wear. He told us the story of the Lakota Thunder Beings, and taught us that dragons are European Thunder Beings.

We like Uncle Roger; he knows we're not stuffed. He invites us to ceremony. He's our uncle you see. So we found him some nice dragon stone too. Just like ours – if you look – you'll see a dragon inside. That's why its magickal. It's not just anyone who can carry a dragon around.

We came off the Caer and went to Cardington for lunch; they serve real cream with the coffee. "Oooo" said Christine. Everything was beyond yummy.

Then we went into a village, Much Wenlock, with the best bakery for miles around. There were dragons and bears, everywhere. I was so happy Christine had made me stay; remember our first night when I wanted to go back?

CHAPTER NINE

Sometime in the following week we headed for the Salisbury Plain. We took the train down through Wales then crossed into England. Seems the tree sprites still breathe in much more than private garden or national park. I saw their wild cousins, gigantic willows hung with lichen, huddling near the southern borderlands – whispering and dancing. Someday I hope they'll speak with me.

On a hillside just outside Bath I saw a great chalk horse who told me of the dragon wars and the sorrow caused in horse kind by people beings. We would see two more chalk horses during our stay – I've heard there are five in England. Ah, but it was Salisbury that captured us now.

We were going to Stonehenge. All the years Christine had lived here, she'd never gone there. Now she was taking us.

A friend of the lady we were staying with in Shropshire met us at the station. After dinner and a gallery exhibit we went out to the stones – a great many of which are Welsh. That has bearing, which in a minute I shall tell.

Christine told me when she was young the Welsh folk taught her to listen to stones. Bluestone they told held all that had gone before and could counsel on what will come. There are ancient songs sung to wake stones and ancient songs sung by those stones to wake others, to call the elements, to conjure magick folk. Wizard kind learned from the stones a magick much older than that known to people kind. That is why in legend they were so revered, and feared.

We went first in the late of night. You could feel them long before you could see them. They breathed on the plain – the monoliths I mean. Not unlike the Welsh mountains actually, for they breathe too I think I forgot to tell you.

It was then I swooned. Too dizzy I felt. My stuffing pulled the rest of me into the circle of stones.

There was one stone in particular, not the largest and not the one with a little one on top of it. I felt like I was right against that one (it was a fat little bluestone – sometimes I'm called a fat little bear). It was time to go sleep and dream, for though I left, part of it became me.

Next morning, just after opening time, we were back. Not more than fifteen people folk were there too. The ravens called us to attention. The stones were singing. "Little ones, I think I need to learn Welsh." Christine said to us. I guess she heard them too.

I listened then Great Mother Bear stretched in that one stone and spoke to me. I learnt of the beginning times and how we came to be. I was led about, in the pack, and watched a country in the stones awake.

Hundreds, maybe thousands of spirit folk reside in each. Many stories they can tell. You must listen close. Not of wizard or dragon kind, or the role of messenger Fay, not even the adventures of heroic grizzly cubs and dragon imps will they only tell.

No, stories too of simple kind you'll hear– with gentle hopes, even tragic dreams. I don't know how long we stayed. The crowd had grown to perhaps a hundred, and a tour bus arrived. The stones were silent now, but their stories still spun all about. It was time to go.

A storm was coming too. We went to Avebury in a downpour – sat in a pub waiting for it to clear. They had great desserts there.

Ooo, there were many more giant bears and dragons, wizards and Goddesses, kings from long ago – all sorts of stuff at Avebury. It goes on for miles, dwarfing Stonehenge. Yes, I made a pun; I want you to figure it out you see.

What first made me happy now made me sad. The stones at Avebury stand within the village. I heard them sing and felt delight. Then I saw bits of them in garden walls and house parts.

Unlike Stonehenge's close circle, Avebury's marching style is easier (less dangerous) to chip apart. So stolen away – recycled shall we say, have been – uh, bits of the monument.

Of course they sing too, though I doubt anyone hears. See, Stonehenge is a famous place – this place, well, not many know about it. Besides, remember how even Stonehenge quieted amidst the chatter?

Well, the Avebury stones live in a village. Still, I was grateful to come and see them and learn about the Council of the Changing. I liked the desserts too.

On our last morning we visited the magnificent Salisbury cathedral (well, tiny, cute and leaning compared to York's). Sorry to say that we were in such a rush we didn't get to play there much.

You see, all the carvings on the outside have tales to tell – not to mention all the curved spaces and secret hollows on the inside. Hearing even some of that, takes time you see. Alas, we had only another week.

Just like in York, Chester and Ludlow too, some of the sprites who helped woodcarver, metal smith, stone mason, tapestry weaver, mosaic or stained glass artisan to create the sacred works, remain inside those works. They are proud, you see, to show them off to you or me. Just ask, you'll see.

Well, Yorkshire loved the gargoyles. He went on a mission to search out every one in just about every medieval building we passed. There are lots of those in Britain. At first I thought he was being silly, or getting me back for all of those Bear's Inns, Cafes and Pubs. Then I realized he was teaching us something.

It was the gargoyles who'd been set to protect, not from evil spirits, but from the forgetfulness of people folk. Today we see how much nastiness forgetfulness brings. In the long ago, each sacred building, great hall or simple home had been made by spirit folk and people kind working together you see. In the Forgetting Times there had to be left a memory of that once upon a time harmony. That memory works like a modern calling card.

Yorkshire had just taught me. Those gargoyles, tapestries, statuary, carvings – all those wondrous things we have not much of across the sea, are the calling cards of magick beings. Just like us, others found ways to obey the Council (shun the people folk), while disobeying too.

It took me running about in Salisbury cathedral, still listening to my favourite Stonehenge stone to understand. Wow - here was another gift of the contrary elves! Nobody would ever guess.

It was in beauty that many stayed. Do you remember? After the Changing not all magick folk ran away. Some remained where they'd always been, some became stuffed, some tiny figures in wood or stone, others became kachinas too. Well, some did a thing even sneakier than Yorkshire and me.

They sprouted from the buildings, art and stories of people kind! They let them think they'd created them. No threat could creations be, just like us who'd become stuffed, you see.

Gargoyles, Green Men, Sprites, Merfolk and Fay watched through dragon wars and dark times too, not by hiding but by standing out, bold in daylight. It was by the strength of their magick that they remained, remained for the day when people folk would see again. We had to hurry now, so I couldn't hear their stories.

CHAPTER TEN

We trained back to Shropshire where we finished the Tales and went onto London. Now our time was really short. We were returning to California in less than a week. I was just learning with whom I wanted to speak. Oh well, there'll be a next time.

In London Christine went to a vellum shop to buy supplies for our illuminated manuscript. She took us to the British Museum. She said we should see something of her mother's folk, the Greeks and Egyptians.

I liked the British Museum. A nice people kind in the cloak room said we could go in and see, instead of staying with all the other cloaks, packages and 'things' he had to oversee.

Oh my, oh my, the Greek people folk painted us and them on fired clay – vases, figures, dinner plates too. They offered us sweets and goodies and knew we were everywhere to be found. They set us in marble, ivory and gold. Then they forgot about us. I wonder why?

Christine took us to see the Elgin Marbles. They show a story told in her ancestors' land (Thessaly) about centaurs and people kind. Once decorating the Parthenon, a temple to the Goddess Athena, I don't really know how, but now their story's in pieces in the British Museum.

Christine took us to look and read the cards below each piece. They told the story of how a war between the people folk and centaurs began. It was not precisely true. Every time Christine read a card, I said 'nuh-uh' and I kept saying 'ah-uh' until she took us out of that room.

"Behave yourself!" Yorkshire snapped.

"Nuh-uh" I replied, and went silent.

"Well, so much for the Elgin Marbles, I see." Christine said, taking us off to the Egyptian wing.

Oooo, thousands of years these statues have stood and still they listen if you speak. Christine took us to honor each of the sacred ones, standing there in cool granite or warm limestone. It felt a bit odd to pay homage in a museum – but better there than not at all.

They knew her I saw, just as Kallisto (the Greek Bear Goddess) knew me and Typhon (the Egyptian Dragon God) knew Yorkshire. The sacred never forgets; it is much older and stronger than the Charm. That is what we must never forget.

We went to the Native American and Meso-American section next. Unfortunately the European was closed for renovations. Yorkshire met the Dragon Lords in yet another form, Quetzecoatl. Suddenly, t'was a pattern I saw.

In all the ancient lands we were known – then forgot. So far as I'd seen, each had their dragon wars, their wizard kind and messenger Fay – each had come to explain us away. Also in each, when the dragon wars ended, they began their slow decline, their separation from us. Worse than toys or playthings, we'd simply never been!

That was the working of the Charm you see. To protect the magick beings from the marauding people folk. I think it fair to say it backfired, causing the mess we see today.

Eeek! This was too complex for me. I knew the world was big, but not this big you see. I was hungry too. Christine wanted to go write in the reading room. We changed her mind and went for lunch.

Then we went to a teddy bear museum in Bethel Green. They were celebrating 100 years of me, though I've been around for much longer than that. I was so happy to see European people kind knew Teddy Roosevelt had not invented me! They remembered the Great Cave Bear, you see. So they were honoring much more than what's cuddly and cute in me.

CHAPTER ELEVEN

The next day we were going to Hyde Park, but ended up in Paris instead. I guess you're used to us changing our plans by now. We took a really fast train, went through a long tunnel and popped up in France. Ooo, I like France too.

The customs kin took one look at Christine's hair (multi-colored) and said: "With hair like that, I don't need to see a passport. Welcome to France." We giggled; they didn't see us. Well, no doubt it was the hair.

"There you go guys. You got me into England; I got you into France." she said laughing. We were visiting Christine's business friends who'd never met us, so we played stuffed. We were placed in the trunk (boot) while the car sped through Paris. I really wanted to see the sights.

Yorkshire started banging on the roof. I told him to stop. He wouldn't listen. The car pulled over. Seems Nicole heard us and knew we wanted to see Paris. She had her husband stop the car and sent Christine to fetch us to the front seat. Nicole is really nice you see.

We went to Sacre Coeur but it was a very hazy November day. Still I was fascinated by the streets, the buildings and the light. It's in many tones and shades and colors at once. No place else has light like that I think. If it does, take me!

"Becoming quite the traveler bear I see." Christine said to me. "No problem. Just fund me and I'll happily escort you all over the globe." she promised us. Yorkshire flapped his wings.

Just then, on the balcony below, we saw a small, veiled pavilion and out came a people kind pretending to be a magick kind. We watched him silently perform. His grace brought a stilling to those rushing about. He captured them to stop and see, to listen very closely. Perhaps Stonehenge needs a resident mime – Avebury can use a troupe!

Back in the car, 'I want to go to Greece', I thought. "Look!" Yorkshire exclaimed. The Eiffel Tower came into view, scintillating with tiny white lights like bubbles escaping a champagne flute.

The Seine flowed icy blue – there was so much color and light! We passed Notre Dame, Yorkshire promised the gargoyles we'd be back – maybe next year to visit and talk.

That night we stayed home and slept. The big people folk went for dinner. We were tired. We'd seen an awful lot, fairly quickly, to comprehend. We happily played stuffed again.

Next day took us to the palace at Versailles. We went late and were treated to sunset over the gardens. It had rained most of the day so the air was crystal, the sky bright turquoise and orange.

Everything was stately and serene; I could see our kind lurking silently all around. Christine ancestors were happy to see her back on French ground too.

Yes, we'd be back I knew. This was the start of a journey, not the ending of one. In less than two days time we were in California again.

The customs kin did not want to let us in! "Where'd you get that?" they pointed at us. "Oh, they were born here. Citizens, you see." Christine said of Yorkshire and me. I longed to go back. Yet I knew something now I hadn't before.

The world is much vaster than the wood where I grew up, than California or America too. No matter where I go, magick folk I find. They flit in shadows, dance in trees, even grace buildings bold as you please.

How can I ever feel lost – alone - or even tossed aside? There are more magick kind than ever I imagined could be. Yorkshire was right. We're a whole world, you see.

So if ever you feel lost, alone, or cast aside, start to look around. More friends than you know you have, you'll find. Don't forget to call on us or magick kind.

Also by Chris Carmines